WILD PAPA WOODS

Written by Patrice Lawrence
Illustrated by Carl Pearce

Contents

Published by Pearson Education Limited, Edinburgh Gate, Harlow, Essex, CM20 2JE.

www.pearsonschools.co.uk

Text © Patrice Lawrence 2013

Designed by Bigtop
Original illustrations © Pearson Education Limited 2013
Illustrated by Carl Pearce, Advocate Illustration Agency

The right of Patrice Lawrence to be identified as author of this work has been asserted
by her in accordance with the Copyright, Designs and Patents Act 1988.

First published 2013

17 16 15 14 13
10 9 8 7 6 5 4 3 2 1

British Library Cataloguing in Publication Data
A catalogue record for this book is available from the British Library

ISBN 978 0 435 14378 7

Printed and bound in the UK by Ashford Colour Press.

Acknowledgements
We would like to thank Bangor Central Integrated Primary School, Northern Ireland;
Bishop Henderson Church of England Primary School, Somerset; Bletchingdon
Parochial Church of England Primary School, Oxfordshire; Brookside Community
Primary School, Somerset; Bude Park Primary School, Hull; Carisbrooke Church
of England Primary School, Isle of Wight; Cheddington Combined School,
Buckinghamshire; Dair House Independent School, Buckinghamshire; Glebe Infant
School, Gloucestershire; Henley Green Primary School, Coventry; Lovelace Primary
School, Surrey; Our Lady of Peace Junior School, Slough; Tackley Church of
England Primary School, Oxfordshire; and Twyford Church of England School,
Buckinghamshire for their invaluable help in the development and trialling of the Bug
Club resources.

Every effort has been made to contact copyright holders of material reproduced in
this book. Any omissions will be rectified in subsequent printings if notice is given to
the publishers.

WILD PAPA WOODS

CHAPTER

A wad of green slime hit Liani's avatar in the middle of its face.

"Got you!" Cyril yelled.

Liani shrugged. "That's lame."

On the screen, a puddle of goo shaped like a cannon fired more balls of slime at her. She wanted to grab her twin brother and shake that smug look off his face, but any more arguments and they'd be in real trouble when Dad came

home from work.

"You stay in if you want," Liani said. "I've got better things to do."

Liani left him to his game and went to find her camera. She preferred taking photographs without Cyril anyway. Yesterday, she'd taken an awesome shot of **bachac** ants marching across Dad's back yard. She planned to send it to her mum who was away teaching at a school in Mombasa, in Kenya; she thought it might remind her of Trinidad.

The camera was charging in the living room. Liani pulled out the cable and turned the camera on. Nothing. She flicked the switch off, then on again. No click, no whir of energy. She checked the cable; it had been unplugged!

"Cyril!" Liani stormed back to his room.

He looked up from his screen. "Back for more green slime?"

"Why did you do that? Only a really mean, fat, stinking toad would be that mean!"

Cyril's mouth fell open. "What?"

"What's all this noise?" Pearl, their stepmother, was in the doorway, her face creased and tired. She tugged down her shirt, but it wouldn't quite cover her pregnant belly. "Please, I need you to be quiet so that I can rest." She ran a hand across her damp face.

Liani glared at Cyril. "He unplugged my camera so it didn't charge!"

Cyril jumped up. "No, I didn't!"

Pearl stepped forward. "No, he didn't." She wiped her forehead; her eyes were all red and puffy.

"It's a really hot day. I needed to plug in the big fan to keep cool."

"But I can't take any photos," Liani protested.

Pearl sighed. "You can plug it in again later."

"But that's not fair ... Pearl? Are you okay?"

Pearl was fanning her face. She staggered forward and then sank onto the bed.

"Is the baby coming?" Cyril's voice was suddenly panicky.

"I don't think so," Liani said, "but go next door and get Mrs Krishnan. Then phone Dad."

Cyril ran out. Liani swallowed hard. "Is it the baby?"

Pearl was breathing hard. "No, but I thought I was going to faint."

Mrs Krishnan came straight away, took one look at Pearl and ushered her into the car to go to hospital. Cyril and Liani stayed next door with Vashikar, Mrs Krishnan's eldest daughter.

"Do you think Pearl will tell Dad it's all *our* fault?" Liani said.

Cyril raised his eyebrows. "*Our* fault?"

"If you hadn't been so horrible to me, we wouldn't have quarrelled," Liani replied.

Cyril began to look uncomfortable too. *Good!* thought Liani.

The twins ran outside as soon as they heard Mrs Krishnan's car pull back up. Dad climbed out and opened his arms, scooping Cyril and Liani towards him. He led them to the swinging sofa in their front garden. "Sorry." Liani stared at Dad's shoes. "I didn't mean to upset Pearl."

"It's not your fault." Dad gave her a little smile. "The pregnancy's been hard for her. Last month, she almost fainted in the bank and they had to call me to take her home. The doctors are keeping her in hospital for a few days, to make sure she and the baby are all right."

"Are you going to stay at home with us more?" Liani asked.

Dad laughed. "I wish I could, but I have to work. I've got a fun idea though ..."

Cyril frowned. "What?"

"How about a couple of weeks staying with your Uncle Ochossi?"

Cyril groaned. "Drop me at the bottom of a snake pit. No, in the middle of a termites' nest. Anything. But please, not there."

But Liani was grinning. "Up in the forest? This is going to be awesome!"

CHAPTER

It was an hour's drive up to Uncle Ochossi's house. Liani was stuck in the back seat. In front, Cyril's headphones were clamped tightly across his head.

The front seat was wasted on Cyril; his eyes were closed most of the time. He was missing the banks of drooping banana trees and the gnarled roots twisting down to the roadside. He didn't hear Dad pointing out the channels where waterfalls flowed, heavier in rainy season.

Peering over the long drop from the side of the road, Liani saw a muddy river, lined with giant bamboo. Her camera was twitching in her lap, but Dad said they had no time to stop.

Uncle Ochossi's house was turquoise, built on squat pillars on a steep slope. Their house in Port of Spain, Trinidad's capital, was locked in a cage, with metal grilles across their door and all the windows.

Uncle's home felt wide open. A small path through an open garden led to steps up to the scarlet front door where Uncle was waiting.

Uncle Ochossi never changed. His grey curly hair and beard were always unruly and spiked with a leaf or two. He was wearing his usual baggy white shirt and faded trousers tucked into his massive boots.

He was holding his arms wide. "Welcome!"

As he hugged her, Liani caught the smell of the forest.

Uncle Ochossi led them into the cool house. A small flight of wooden stairs led up to the room beneath the roof, where Uncle had set out two camp beds, separated by a curtain.

"Look!" Liani flung open the window and turned to her brother. "You can see right over the forest!"

"No, thanks." Cyril flopped on his bed.

"What are you going to do?"

"Nothing."

"Isn't that boring?"

"No TV. No internet. *That*'s boring!"

"Uncle's going to roast **breadfruit** for us later. Help us collect wood for the fire."

"Yeah! And be dinner for the mosquitoes?" Cyril quipped. "No, thank you."

Cyril's voice had a little shake to it. Liani bit back her annoyance. She was always telling people that twins didn't automatically know what the other was thinking, but she knew Cyril better than anyone.

She sat on his bed. "I miss Mum too."

Cyril gave her a funny look. "Why are you talking about Mum?"

"Sometimes I wish she hadn't gone to Kenya."

Cyril sighed. "Me too. I hate being stuck here. There's no internet, so we can't even see her."

"Internet?" Uncle Ochossi had climbed the wooden steps without a sound. He was carrying a fat breadfruit. "I don't need the internet myself, but my friend Mr Eugene has a café full of computers."

"An internet café?" Cyril propped himself up on one arm.

"Just down the road." Uncle Ochossi smiled. "Shall we visit him tomorrow?"

Cyril nodded so hard Liani worried his head would fly off and bounce out of the window.

Uncle Ochossi held out the breadfruit. "Ready to see it roast?"

They lit small, round lanterns to light the way down the slope. The bonfire glowed in the clearing before the undergrowth plaited itself together.

The twins sat on stools by the fire, sipping **cocoa tea**, the cinnamon tingling in the back of their throats.

Uncle stared thoughtfully at the black forest. "He's probably watching us, but he never shows himself, not unless his friends are in danger."

Liani leaned forward to catch his voice above the crackly wood. "Who, Uncle?"

Poking the blackening breadfruit with a stick, Uncle explained.

"They call him Papa Bois. He came from the ancient forests, long before the first people. He knows every thorn and every root. He knows each of the birds by name and every single butterfly by the flutter of its wings against his face. For thousands of years, he has walked these lands, protecting nature."

"What does he look like?" Cyril asked.

Uncle jabbed the breadfruit so it rolled out of the fire towards them. It looked like an old cannonball. "Nobody knows for sure. Legend says he's an old African man, but he's stronger than Superman, with hooves to chase his enemies. Sometimes, they say, he changes shape, becoming part of the forest itself. But you mustn't worry. The forest is a safe place if you are Papa Bois's friend."

A log popped in the fire, sending out a spray of sparks. Uncle cut the steaming breadfruit into chunks and handed them around. Liani gazed into the dark undergrowth. Perhaps hidden eyes were staring back.

CHAPTER 3

Next morning, Cyril's voice was groggy on the other side of the curtain.

"Someone needs to reset that cockerel," he groaned, sleepily.

Liani stretched. "It's only doing what it's supposed to do."

The camp bed squeaked as Cyril moved about. "I don't care! I'm not getting up yet."

Liani dressed, found her camera and headed downstairs. Uncle Ochossi was sitting on the balcony, but not alone. A tiny emerald hummingbird was hovering around his face, so close it almost landed on his ear. Liani switched on her camera and raised the viewer to her eye.

Heavy footsteps thumped down behind her. Cyril was muttering. "If I catch that cockerel …" Liani held up her hand. "Shush!"

"Now what?"

"Too late!"

The bird flew away and Uncle came in, silent as a feather in his clumsy boots. His eyes glinted amber in the morning light.

After breakfast, Uncle took Liani and Cyril down to Mr Eugene's.

"Bushpapa!" Mr Eugene slapped Uncle on the back. "So pleased to meet your family at last!"

Liani laughed. "Bushpapa?"

"He hasn't told you?" Mr Eugene grinned. "He's the king of the forest!"

Uncle Ochossi shook his head, smiling. "Not now, Mr Eugene!"

"He's too modest!" Mr Eugene said. "Children, come with me."

To Liani's surprise, they passed through the café to a computer in Mr Eugene's office. When Mr Eugene nudged the mouse, the screensaver cleared to show a person waving at them.

"Mum!" Liani yelled.

"The connection is good," Mr Eugene said. "Take as long as you like."

That afternoon, Cyril stopped sulking; he was happy helping Uncle with chores while Liani stalked a pair of **kiskadees**. They were teasing her, perched in an old nutmeg tree, but every time she lifted her camera, they fluttered away.

She focussed the lens, and was about to take the shot, when suddenly a shriek ripped through the air. *Cyril?* Liani raced up to the house and found her brother standing under the jut of the balcony floor, mouth open, staring at a bucket.

Liani was furious. "You're afraid of a bucket?" She kicked it aside, and … Oh! That's what Cyril was staring at – sludge-coloured skin, a pale, fat belly.

"**Crapaud**!" she whispered.

The enormous toad looked right back at them and flicked out its tongue.

"Uncle!" she yelled.

He appeared round the side of the house. "What's wrong?"

"Salt!" Liani ordered. "Bring some quick!"

Uncle frowned. "Salt?"

"It's a crapaud," Cyril pointed. "There!"

"You want me to help you torture that poor creature?" Uncle's voice sounded like a growl. He scooped up the toad and placed it inside the bucket. "Let me take you home." He picked up the bucket. "You two, come with me!"

They followed Uncle past the ashes of last night's fire and into the undergrowth.

Uncle Ochossi turned to Cyril. "What's wrong with Mr Crapaud?"

Cyril eyed the bucket warily. "He's seriously ugly," he chuckled.

Uncle nodded. "Some might agree. But I've seen people uglier than that."

Cyril sniggered. "Well, this teacher ..."

Liani nudged him. "Shush!"

Uncle turned to her. "And you, Miss Photographer, what's your reason?"

"A crapaud nearly killed Grandma's dog."

Uncle laughed. "Well if some slobbering beast tried to bite *you*, wouldn't you complain?"

Liani looked thoughtful. "Well …"

"Mr Crapaud only uses poison to defend himself. He didn't invite the dog to chew him."

They were following a path between a stream and a wall of giant bamboo. Uncle held up the bucket. "Nearly there, my friend." He squinted ahead. "What's going on?"

A circle of bamboo had been hacked away and scraps of plastic were caught between the stubs. Fast food boxes were piled up next to scrunched-up napkins and empty cans.

Uncle Ochossi touched the sharp edges of the broken bamboo. "Hunters. In my forest."

He picked up the bucket and gently tipped out the toad. Standing up slowly, he cocked his head, as if straining to hear. To Liani's shock, he suddenly started to run, tearing through the bush, silent in his heavy boots.

Liani grabbed Cyril's arm. "Come on!"

They stumbled after him, catching flashes of his white shirt through the trees until he came to a stop in a small clearing.

"I think he's with something," Liani whispered, her excitement rising as she peered through forest undergrowth.

"It's a deer," Cyril said.

The animal was sprawled on its side, legs splayed awkwardly, its body juddering as it tried to breathe. As they drew closer, Liani saw the dark wound on its flank.

Uncle was sitting by it, stroking its head. His mouth was moving, though Liani couldn't hear words. Gradually, the deer's breathing became calmer, until finally it was still.

Uncle looked up angrily.

"Hunters. In my forest."

They walked back to the house in silence. After supper, Uncle sat on the balcony, staring out over the forest. He was still there when Liani went to bed. She half-expected to see him the next morning, but when she went downstairs he was gone.

"He's clearing up the forest." Cyril frowned at the scratchy handwriting on Uncle's note. "He said we should go down to Mr Eugene's."

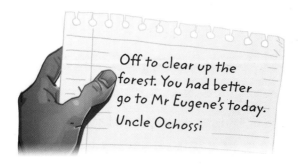

Liani leaned over the balcony rail and looked out over the forest. Uncle was somewhere beneath the tangle of trees, clearing up the soggy rubbish by himself.

Cyril joined her. "We're not going to
Mr Eugene's café, are we?"

"No." Liani replied.

They left the house quickly. As they traced a
path through the undergrowth, Liani imagined the
trees bending into each other, planning mischief.

"Are you sure this is the right way?" Cyril asked.

"I think so. Listen, can you hear the stream?"

Cyril stood still, concentrating. "I think I can
hear parrots."

"Parrots?" Liani listened hard. There was
something, but it didn't sound like a parrot.

They weaved their way through the bushes,
towards the noise.

Liani pointed. "It's coming from there."

A small wire cage at the bottom of a tree was
rocking hard as its occupant threw itself about.
Tufts of blonde fur clumped through the gaps and,
as they watched, a tiny hand grabbed at the trap.

"It's a monkey," Liani said. "We can't leave it
in there!"

Cyril backed away. "It's going to bite our faces
as soon as we open the door."

Liani bent down for a closer look. The monkey was gnawing hopelessly at the wire. But it wasn't alone. Big eyes in a tiny heart-shaped face stared back. "It's got a baby!" she cried.

The camera was dangling from Liani's wrist.

"Cyril, open the cage!" she demanded.

"No. I want to keep my face."

"And I want to take an action shot as they escape!"

Cyril shook his head.

Liani sighed. "Look at that baby! The hunters are probably going to take it away from its mum and sell it."

The monkey crouched, exhausted in the cage, its baby behind it, shivering.

"You could use a stick to open the latch," Liani suggested.

Cyril sighed. "Okay, but it has to be a really long stick."

While Liani crouched in position with her camera, Cyril jabbed the lock until it sprang away from the door. As the monkeys shot out across the forest floor, Liani pressed the shutter on her camera again and again.

"That's why I like computer games," Cyril said. "I'm in charge of the surpri ..." Cyril's mouth snapped shut. Liani turned around. Two men stared back at her. One was tall with heavy shoulders, a green cap shading his eyes. The shorter one wore army trousers, with a bulging sports bag thrown over his shoulder. They stomped towards Liani and Cyril, their boots crushing the ferns.

The tall one pointed to the trap. "Did you open that?"

Cyril answered. "It was just a monkey and her baby."

The men's eyes widened and the tall one said, "Do you know how much money they pay for a baby?"

Above them, the trees were whispering again, but from deeper in the forest came a different sound. Like a trumpet, Liani thought.

The hunters looked around nervously. The short one shrugged. "It's nothing."

His companion grinned. "You think that's nothing too?"

Liani stared at where the man was pointing. A stag stood, just a few metres away, studying them. It lowered its head, showing off its moss-grey antlers. She raised her camera and took a quick shot.

The short hunter unzipped his bag and pulled out a length of rope. "Why are we chasing monkeys when we could catch one of these?"

The stag lifted its head and fixed its golden eyes on Liani. It turned around slowly, but didn't move away. The hunters smiled at each other and started creeping towards it.

"Run," Liani said, under her breath. The hunters were now so close to the stag they could almost touch it. It trotted away through the forest, just ahead of them until they were all out of sight.

"Why doesn't the stag run faster?" Cyril asked. "Is he wounded?"

"It's strange," Liani said. "It's almost teasing them. We'd better get out of here, though, in case they come back."

Cyril and Liani were turning to go when BANG! Suddenly the forest was all movement, stirred by ripples of air.

"They killed the stag!" Liani looked for Cyril, but he was already ahead of her, racing back towards the noise.

"There!" Cyril gasped, pointing.

The hunters were stumbling through the trees towards them. The short one was limping, his trousers ripped at the knee. His companion cradled his elbow in his hand, a ragged scratch across his cheek. They stopped, back to back, circling round.

The short one flapped at the air, his eyes wide with terror.

"Show yourself!" he cried. Then suddenly, he lurched away, with the tall one following.

Cyril scratched his head. "What was that all about?"

"No idea," Liani said.

"Liani? Cyril?" Uncle's familiar voice was calling out from behind a silk cotton tree. They found him sitting against the tree trunk, tucking his trousers into his boots. He stood up slowly, rubbing his back.

"What are you doing here, Uncle Ochossi?" Cyril asked.

"The same as you. I heard a noise." Uncle plucked a leaf from his beard. "But I was too late."

Liani's stomach flopped. "Did they kill the stag?"

Uncle shook his head. "No, the stag's safe. I was too late because you stopped them first."

Cyril laughed. "No we didn't! That stag came and then … then what happened? Those hunters were terrified!"

Uncle's eyes glowed amber. "Perhaps they found that the forest has friends."

"Yes," Liani agreed.

But her eyes were on his feet. As Uncle bent to stand up, she was sure she'd seen it. The shape of his feet beneath the rubber boots. Small, curved and solid, like hooves.

SPIDER FACE

CHAPTER

Cyril and Liani were going to travel the world. Last year, while their mum was teaching at a school in Kenya, they had spent most of their summer holidays with their mysterious Uncle Ochossi high up in the hill forests of Trinidad. This summer holiday, though, was special. Not only was Mum around, but she was also making up for being away last year by taking them on a big trip to Kenya.

It was an uncomfortable night on the plane to Nairobi, Kenya's capital city. Liani was sitting in-between Cyril and Mum, chattering on about all the animals she was planning to photograph. Even when the lights dimmed and the other passengers covered themselves with blankets, Liani was crouched forward over her table making notes. It's going to be a long night, Cyril thought. Very long indeed.

When they arrived in Nairobi, the journey wasn't over. They had to hang around and catch another plane. Their final destination was the island of Lamu, just off the east coast of Kenya. There they'd be staying with Astra, who'd been a teacher with Mum the previous summer.

"Astra's shown me so many pictures," Mum said. "Lamu looks like something out of a film!"

Cyril tried hard to be enthusiastic, but he couldn't understand what all the fuss was about. He'd lived his whole life in Trinidad. Surely an island was just an island? If it was a floating mountain or a giant, drifting iceberg – now that really would be something to be excited about. At least he'd brought a good supply of computer games ...

Liani didn't share Mum's excitement either.

"So there aren't any lions?"

Mum rolled her eyes. "I've already told you, Liani. No lions. No elephants. No hippos."

"Not even a giraffe?"

"I know you and your Uncle Ochossi love nature, but I wish you'd just calm down a little."

Liani slumped back, sulking. Mum looked very relieved when they were finally called for their flight.

CHAPTER

Mum tried to convince Cyril that small planes were as safe as big planes, but Cyril couldn't relax until they landed at the airport on Manda, the island next to Lamu. From there, they were led along a narrow wooden jetty to a boat taking them out through the mangroves across the bay to Lamu Port. Liani peered into the water looking for fish, while Cyril kept looking straight ahead towards the approaching town. Cyril felt nervous as the small boat bobbed up and down across the deep bay.

At last, they reached the other side. As the boat weaved through the crowd of vessels at the port, Mum scanned the wharf.

"There she is," Mum pointed. "That's Astra!"

The boatmen secured the boat, helping the passengers onto the jetty and up the steep stairs to the waterfront.

Mum was hugging a tall woman wearing a bright patterned scarf over her hair and strings of beads round her wrists.

"We've been looking forward to staying with you so much," said Mum.

Astra grinned. "I've been looking forward to it too. And these are your little ones?"

"Not so little," Mum sighed. "One minute they're babies and the next minute they're twelve years old."

Astra turned to the twins. "I bet you've been so excited about coming to Lamu."

Mum gave Liani and Cyril a fierce look.

"Yes," Liani said. "We're really excited."

"Thank you," Cyril added.

Astra looked delighted. "Well, let's go then!"

As Astra and Mum strode off ahead, Cyril whispered to Liani, "Do you think the car's parked nearby?"

Liani laughed so loudly that Mum looked back, frowning at them.

"How many cars can you see?" Liani asked.

"There's … " Cyril stopped. No cars at all. Instead, there were donkeys. Everywhere. They were tethered at the roadside, or trotting past with bags strapped to their sides. Cyril watched one man leading a donkey with a child perched on it. It was like being on another planet where donkeys outnumbered humans.

"This way," Mum called.

They turned away from the waterfront, down a narrow alley where the buildings leaned closer together, and then on to the main street. Cyril was used to seeing different types of people at home in Trinidad, but Lamu was different again. He saw a man draped in red – a **Masai** warrior – just like he had seen on television. Men with colourful **kikoy** sarongs wrapped around their waists sat outside shops. Cyril smiled as he saw one young man wearing a blue and yellow wrap with a football shirt. The women and girls rushed past in long, black robes, their hair and sometimes their faces covered.

Turning off the main street, the passage became even narrower. As they squeezed past a donkey tied to a post, something else caught Cyril's attention.

"Liani? Have you noticed the cats?"

The animals were grouped in doorways and prowling the channels that ran down the side of the street.

"There're millions of them!" Liani said. "But they're a bit weird-looking."

Cyril studied them more closely. Their legs and bodies were more spindly than those of the cats in Trinidad and their ears a bit pointier, like bats'.

The twins caught up with Astra. "Who do all these cats belong to?" Liani asked.

"Everybody and nobody," Astra replied. "The legend is that they're descended from ancient Egyptian cats and travelled with Arabian traders on their **dhows**. This way!"

She led them through a small stone archway into a shady courtyard surrounded by the white walls of the house.

"You'll be staying up here," she said.

The family followed Astra up a flight of stone stairs, past wicker chairs on a rooftop courtyard and up more stairs to a big, wooden door.

"I hope this is okay," Astra said.

The bedroom was vast, with a marble floor and a high ceiling fitted with fans. The three beds were four posters with carved wooden headboards and drooping net curtains. Liani immediately dropped her bags and grabbed her camera to take photos.

"These are traditional Swahili beds," Astra said.

Cyril was impressed; Swahili people really knew how to keep the bugs out at night! But as he looked round the room, he was bothered by something.

"Where's the television?"

Liani rolled her eyes. "Cyril!"

"I'm so sorry, Astra," Mum said. "This is just perfect."

Astra put a hand on Cyril's shoulder. "We don't have a TV because people usually come here for peace." She smiled. "But not everybody. So we do have wireless internet, if that helps."

Cyril grinned. That was more like it.

"I'll leave you to unpack," Astra said, "but your mum and I were talking. How about celebrating your arrival with a sunset sail across the bay? My friend Idarus has a dhow and he's happy to take us out tonight. Does that sound like a good idea?"

"Yes!" Liani said. "Definitely!"

More bobbing around on a tiny boat, Cyril thought. Definitely not.

CHAPTER

The waterfront was still busy in the evening. Traders pulling handcarts offered green coconuts and oranges. Small boats dropped off passengers, and donkeys carried their loads towards the old town, while men sat outside cafés looking on.

Astra pointed. "There's our dhow for tonight."

"Wow!" Liani said. "That's so cool!"

Cyril nodded. His sister was right, for once. It wasn't bad at all. The dhow was much bigger than he'd imagined and its glossy wooden sides were decorated with carvings, including a wooden eye either side of the prow.

Astra's friend, Idarus, helped them on to the boat and introduced them to the two other sailors.

"There's a downstairs, too," Astra said.

She showed them the way down the hatch to a small, cosy cabin below. Its seats were covered in kikoy fabric and a low table was laid out with jugs of juice and oranges.

Liani took one glance and raced back up on to the deck. "I'm going to stay up here!" she said. "I want to take photos of everything!"

"I think I'll join her," Mum said. "What about you, Cyril? Are you coming?"

He dropped his jumper on the sofa. Yes! He was!

The engine whirred into life and the breeze nudged the tall sail. The sky was turning pink as the sun started to set. In the town, the **muezzins** were calling the people to prayer, their sing-song voices wafting from the mosques' **minarets**. Cyril sat back and closed his eyes. Okay, maybe sometimes the outdoors could be fun.

The boat tacked around the dark lagoon, anchoring in the middle as the sun finally dropped behind the horizon, the port just tiny dots of light in the distance.

Cyril rubbed his arms. The evening was cooler now and it was time to put a jumper on.

He climbed down to the cabin. His jumper had been on that cushion. No, there it was, trailed over the boots in the corner. As he bent down to pick it up, the sleeve moved. Cyril jumped back. Rats! Didn't they live on boats?

A hand reached from behind Cyril and gently lifted the jumper.

"There you are." Idarus wasn't talking to Cyril but the creature – no, creatures – beneath Cyril's jumper. Two tiny kittens were nestling up to a thin grey cat.

"The mother's called Mweza," Idarus said. "It means 'moon' in Swahili. She's a street cat who must have been looking for somewhere safe to have her kittens. There were four kittens at first, then three …" He carefully lifted one of the furry scraps away from its mother. Its head sagged against its neck and it gave a weak little cry. "Maybe this one will live, but I'm not sure."

"I don't think so," Astra said, coming down the stairs with Mum and Liani. "I think it's cat flu and once they have that, there's little you can do."

Cyril stroked the kitten's tiny head. "Why don't we take it to a vet?"

Astra and Idarus glanced at each other. "She's too sick now," Astra said. "Many of the cats die because people haven't got the money to vaccinate them. And those are just the ones that belong to someone – most cats don't. The free clinic in the town does the best it can, but you've seen how many cats there are – there's not enough money."

Idarus lay the cat back down by its mother.

"Do the kittens have names?" Cyril asked.

Astra smoothed Mweza's fur. "Not yet. We were waiting to see who survived."

"I think you should give them names anyway," Cyril said.

"Okay," Astra said. "What about this tiny one?"

It was lying still as if even the effort of breathing was tiring it out.

"I think we should call it something that encourages it," Liani said. "What about 'Survivor'?"

Idarus nodded. "In Swahili, 'survivor' is 'nusura'."

"Yes, that sounds like a good name," Liani said. "Nusura."

"And what about this other one?" Idarus lifted the other kitten. It arched its back, trying to twist and bite Idarus's finger.

"It's all squirmy, like a snake," Liani said.

"Kijoja," Idarus said. "That's a little snake."

Cyril studied the kitten's face. It was a strange face, pale grey with a splodge of black fur in the middle and thin streaks of black trailing out across its cheeks and forehead.

"It looks like a spider," Cyril said. "What's the Swahili word for 'spider'?"

"Buibui," Astra said. "That's one of the first Swahili words I learnt."

Idarus placed Buibui back by Mweza and the kitten immediately started to nose around for milk. Nusura didn't move.

Cyril looked at Mum. "There must be something we can do for Nusura."

"She looks very weak," Mum hesitated. "I'm not sure if we can help."

Cyril picked up the kitten and wrapped her in his jumper. "I'll look after Nusura tonight," he insisted, "and tomorrow we'll take her to the vet." Once they were back at the house, Astra found an empty box and lined it with newspapers and rags. Cyril filled a bowl with water and milk and tried to drip it into Nusura's mouth. Liani sat beside them, taking photos and stroking the kitten's head. When Mum insisted that Cyril try to sleep, he placed the box with the kittens and their mother on the bed next to him and pulled the curtains around them. Nusura's eyes flickered.

"Hold on until morning," Cyril said, stroking Nusura's thin body.

CHAPTER

Next morning, Cyril opened his eyes as daylight filtered through the bed's curtains. He reached for the box by his pillow, then sat bolt upright. The box was gone.

He jumped out of bed. "Mum? Liani?"

Seeing their beds were empty, Cyril ran down to the courtyard. Mum and Liani were sitting at a table, their breakfasts barely touched in front of them. Liani looked as though she'd been crying.

"What happened?" Cyril asked.

"I woke up early this morning, when the mosques were calling people to pray," said Mum. "I thought I'd check on Nusura, but … she just wasn't strong enough."

Mum opened her arms to hug Cyril, but he turned and ran back up the steps.

Liani called, "Where are you going?"

"To play on my computer where *I* decide what happens."

Back in his room, Cyril turned on his laptop and clicked through the photos from last summer: Bushpapa's turquoise house ...

... a pair of **kiskadees** in the nutmeg tree.

Liani had even taken a sneaky picture of Bushpapa's boots, because she was convinced he was really Papa Bois – the mythical guardian of the forest.

The door opened. "Are you okay, Cyril?"

"Yes," he said. "I'm fine."

"Let me know if you need anything." He heard Mum's footsteps trail away down the steps. Cyril minimised the photos and opened a game.

He must have dozed off, because he was jerked awake by Liani shaking his shoulders.

"I have to show you something," she said.

"Go away!" he growled.

She was waving her camera around his face. "But you have to look at this!"

He sat up. "Okay, show me your pictures, but don't expect me to be interested."

Cyril turned away from his sister, but she wasn't getting the message. He felt her sit down on the bed, where Nusura's box had been.

"Look!" She held the camera up to Cyril.

He yawned, much louder and wider than he needed to. "Please just go away."

She made a face at him and went back to scrolling through the pictures.

"Just one look." She pushed the camera towards Cyril.

He stared at the image. "Is that …?"

"Yes. That's Buibui."

The tiny cat with the spider face was standing on the dhow deck glaring at the camera like he wanted to pick a fight with it.

"I tried to pick him up and he gave me this," Liani said, showing Cyril a small scratch mark across the back of her hand. "He's tough. But look, there's more."

On the screen, three of the strange-looking cats were sitting on a chair outside a grocery shop. One of them had a brown smudge across his chin as if he'd been eating chocolate. The next photo was a kitten sticking its face out from a gap in a stone wall.

Cyril passed the camera back to Liani. "They're great photos. Now leave me alone."

"Is that all you've got to say?" Liani clicked right back to a picture she'd taken of Nusura

curled up in the corner of the box. "I'm sorry we couldn't save her, but there are hundreds more kittens that maybe we *can* help."

Cyril looked dubious. "How? Just by taking their photos?"

"Yes."

Cyril shook his head and turned back to his laptop. "Good luck."

"Not just taking their photos," Liani said. "But I thought maybe a blog too."

Cyril looked up, suddenly curious. "A blog?"

"Yes! People love looking at cute animals. Some clips get millions of hits. I thought we could do a blog from Buibui's point of view."

"A Buibui blog?" Cyril frowned.

"I suppose you think it's a stupid idea," Liani said.

"No, it's a great idea. I was just thinking about how we could set up the blog. We'd need a 'donate' button so that people could give money, and regular updates …"

Cyril's mind was busy working away.

Their work was set for the rest of the week. Cyril's office was the courtyard, uploading Liani's pictures as she brought them along. Mum helped write the blog entries and Astra and Idarus made sure there were plenty of photos of Buibui, who seemed to have made himself the dhow captain.

On the third day, Astra rushed into the courtyard, grinning. "I've just seen the vet," she said. "There's already enough money from your blog to vaccinate at least fifty cats!"

"That's great!" Liani beamed.

Cyril looked up from the laptop. "How many cats are there in Lamu?"

Astra looked sheepish. "About four thousand. But fifty's a good start," she added, brightly.

"It is," Cyril said. "But even if we raise enough money to vaccinate two hundred cats, that still leaves loads."

"And what's going to happen when we leave?" Liani asked. "Nobody's going to read the blog if it isn't updated."

"That's a good point," Mum said. "I know Buibui wants to rule the dhow, but even he can't write his own blog."

"We could always update it from home," Liani suggested.

Cyril shook his head. "It's not the same."

Astra sank down on the seat, fanning herself. She turned to Mum suddenly with an idea. "Remember when we finished teaching last year? The headmaster, Mr Angwangu, said he owed us a favour."

Liani looked confused. "But he's in Mombasa. How's he going to help?"

"Well, he comes over to Lamu all the time because his eldest son works in one of the hotels," Astra said.

Mum continued. "Even more importantly, he has a school full of children who want to learn English. It's an ideal project for them. They can use their skills and raise money for the clinic at the same time by updating the blog with Mr Angwangu's photographs!"

Liani kissed Mum's cheek. "You're brilliant!"

Mum laughed. "Well, Uncle Ochossi would be proud."

Cyril kissed his mum's other cheek, then grinned at Liani. "You're just like Uncle Ochossi. A real legend!"

bachac – leaf-cutting ant

breadfruit – large, rough-skinned fruit with a bread-like taste and texture

cocoa tea – hot chocolate made from dried cocoa beans and spices

crapaud – toad, pronounced 'crappo'

dhow – traditional sailing boat with a big triangular sail

kikoy – brightly-coloured, patterned cloth which is often used to make clothes

kiskadee – flycatcher bird with a call that sounds like its name

Masai – Kenyan warrior community, usually wearing distinctive red robes

minaret – tower of a mosque from where the muezzin calls people to pray

muezzin – person chosen by a mosque to call worshippers to prayer